HOW TO TAKE CARE OF YOUR PET
DINOSAUR

YOUR PET
PTERODACTYL

By Kirsty Holmes

THE
OFFICIAL
F.O.S.S.I.L
GUIDE

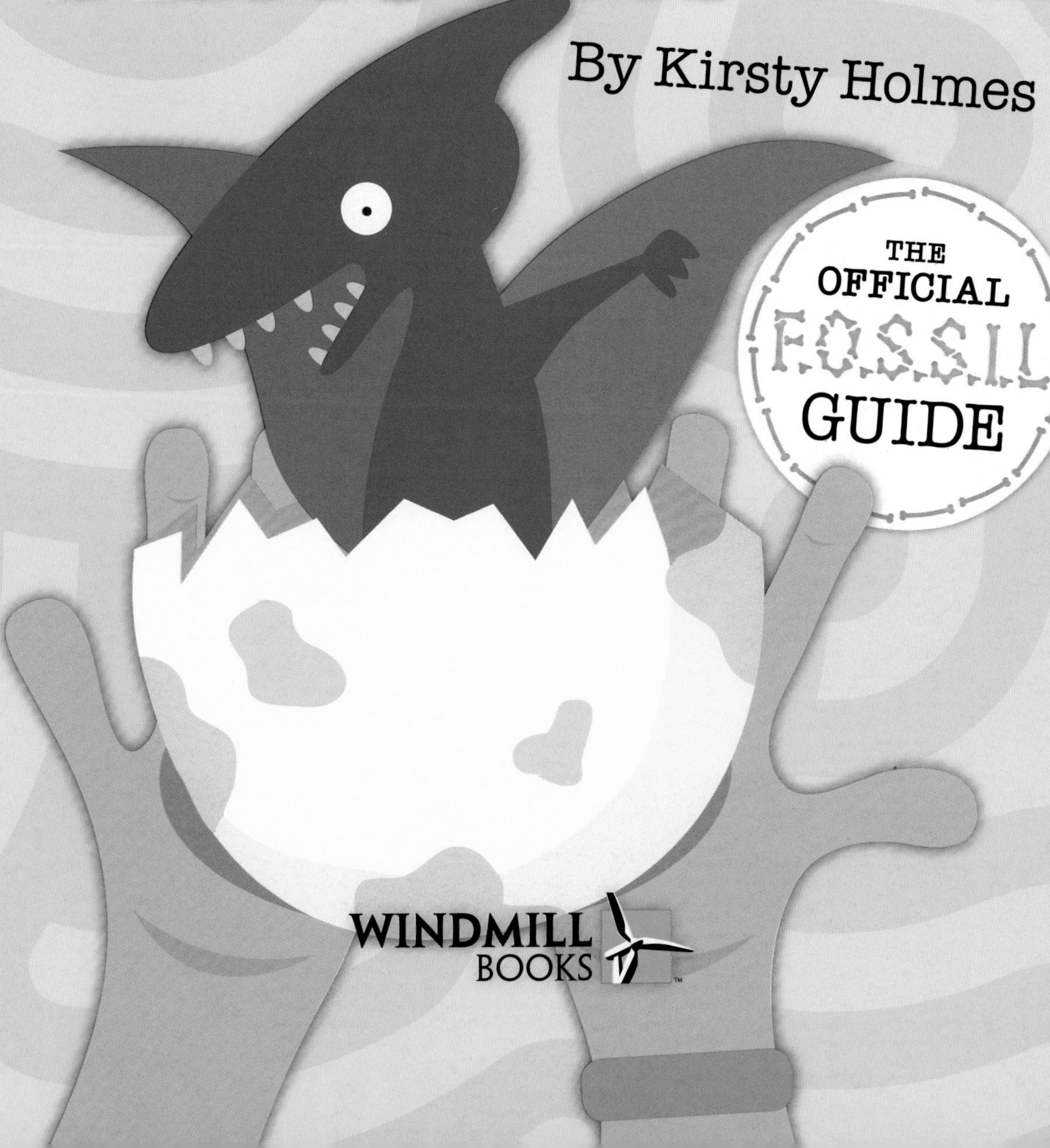

WINDMILL
BOOKS

Published in 2019 by Windmill Books,
an Imprint of Rosen Publishing
29 East 21st Street, New York, NY 10010

© 2019 Booklife Publishing
This edition is published by
arrangement with Booklife Publishing

Editor: Madeline Tyler
Book Design: Danielle Jones

Cataloging-in-Publication Data

Names: Holmes, Kirsty.
Title: Your pet pterodactyl / Kirsty
Holmes.
Description: New York : Windmill Books,
2019. | Series: How to care for your pet
dinosaur | Includes glossary and index.
Identifiers: ISBN 9781538391075 (pbk.)
| ISBN 9781508197607 (library bound) |
ISBN 9781538391082 (6 pack)
Subjects: LCSH: Pterodactyls--Juve-
nile literature. | Dinosaurs--Juvenile
literature.
Classification: LCC QE862.P7 H645 2019
| DDC 567.918--dc2

Manufactured in the United States of
America

CPSIA Compliance Information: Batch
BW19WM: For Further Information contact
Rosen Publishing, New York, New York at
1-800-237-9932

IMAGE CREDITS

CONTENTS

THE OFFICIAL F.O.S.S.I.L GUIDE

Words that look like this can be found in the glossary on page 24.

F.O.S.S.I.L

So, you're the proud owner of a pterodactyl egg. Congratulations!

Owning a pet pterodactyl is a lot of hard work, but it's worth the trouble. Pterodactyls make excellent pets.

Per 1
Gn +1
C6/M7
P5/E2
M1 1.3

CONGRATULATIONS!
IT'S A ... PTERODACTYL!

Pterodactyls (say: ter-uh-DAK-tills) are not technically dinosaurs. They are actually flying reptiles, known as pterosaurs, from the same <u>era</u> as the dinosaurs. Don't worry, though, F.O.S.S.I.L still has a book on how to take care of them.

F.O.S.S.I.L FACT

F.O.S.S.I.L stands for:

Federal
Office of
Super
Sized
Interesting
Lovable reptiles

HOW TO TAKE CARE OF YOUR PET
DINOSAUR
YOUR PET
PTERODACTYL
THE OFFICIAL F.O.S.S.I.L GUIDE

EGGS

Pterodactyl eggs are quite small, with soft shells. They are about 1.5 inches (4 cm) long, and 1.2 inches (3 cm) across. The eggs weigh around 0.2–0.4 ounce (6–11 g).

Pterodactyl eggs have soft shells and <u>absorb</u> nutrients and moisture from the ground.

THE BEST PLACE TO KEEP YOUR EGG IS IN AN UNDERGROUND <u>NEST.</u>

BABIES

Pterodactyl babies are known as "flaplings." Flaplings are very small when they first hatch.

Some flaplings will be able to fly as soon as they hatch. Others will need more care, and you will need to bring them food and teach them to fly.

GROWTH

Your flapling will grow slowly and steadily.

FIRST YEAR

Skull: 1.8 inches (4.6 cm)
Teeth: 15
Wings: 8 inches (20 cm)

SECOND YEAR

Skull: 3.7 inches (9.4 cm)
Teeth: 30–60
Wings: 16–24 inches (41–61 cm)

THIRD YEAR

Skull: 10.6 inches (27 cm)
Teeth: 90
Wings: 5 feet (1.5 m)

The biggest type of pterosaur is called Quetzalcoatlus
(say: qwet-zul-co-at-las). It grows as tall as a giraffe.
If your egg hatches into one of these, we suggest getting
some specialist advice.

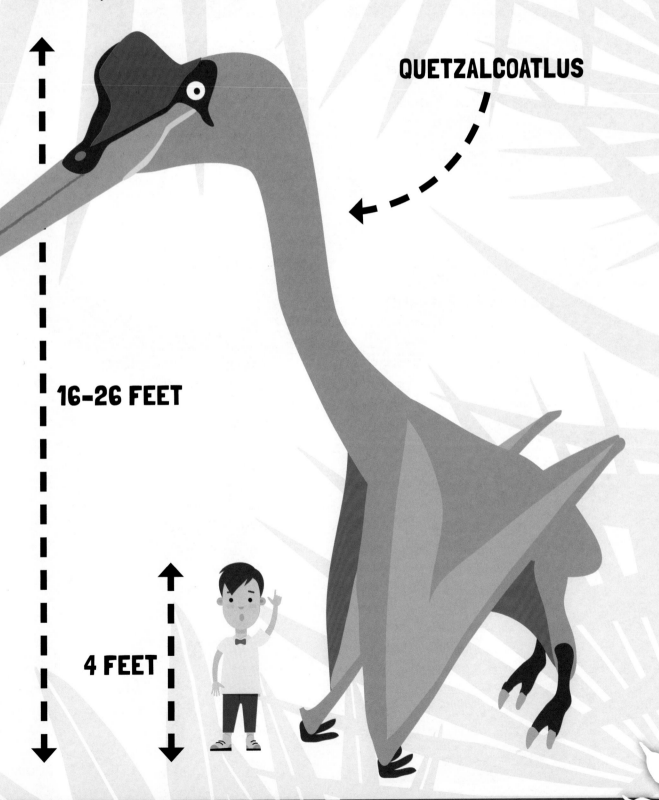

QUETZALCOATLUS

16-26 FEET

4 FEET

FOOD

Pterodactyls are <u>predators</u>. They have mouths full of sharp teeth, perfect for catching fish. They hunt by swooping down to the sea and snapping the fish in their teeth.

FISH

SQUID

SHELLFISH

CRABS

Pterodactyls that live by the sea eat fish and shellfish. Pterodactyls that live <u>inland</u> eat insects, eggs, and meat. Sometimes they also eat fruit.

EXERCISE

Your pterodactyl can fly a long way – some can fly for days without stopping. This means you will need to give your pet plenty of exercise and let it out regularly to stretch its wings.

HOME!

Pterosaurs have quite large brains and can be very clever. Teach your pterosaur some simple but important commands to control its behavior when outdoors.

NAMING

Naming your pterosaur is very important when <u>bonding</u> with your pet. You could choose to use part of the pterosaur's name as a nickname.

F.O.S.S.I.L FACT

If your pet misbehaves, call it by its full name: Pterrence.

Pterry

You could use words that describe your pterodactyl to name it instead.

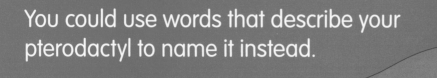

THIS OWNER NAMED HIS PET "FLAPPY" BECAUSE OF ITS AMAZING WINGS.

FLAPPY!

FOSSIL FACT

What will you name your pterodactyl?

WASHING

Pets must be kept clean and well groomed. Pterodactyls can end up with a lot of small insects stuck to them after a flight. To properly clean your pet, you will need:

GOGGLES

POLISH

GLOVES

A SCRUBBING BRUSH

A SOFT CLOTH

Make sure to distract your pet while washing. Its teeth are very sharp! F.O.S.S.I.L suggests using a treat or toy.

19

PROBLEMS

Keeping your pterodactyl indoors for too long can result in damage to your furniture and curtains.

MAKE SURE YOUR PET IS LET OUT EVERY DAY, OR IS KEPT OUTSIDE IN AN <u>AVIARY</u>.

Storms, thunder, lightning, and wind can all be dangerous for a pterodactyl. Make sure you keep your pet safe in bad weather.

TRICKS

Teach your pterodactyl some flying tricks and have fun while exercising your pet. Tricks such as dive-bombs and loop-the-loops will impress your friends and entertain your pet.

MAKE SURE TO GIVE YOUR PET A TREAT WHEN IT DOES WELL.

Get together with your friends and their pterodactyls and you could even teach them to fly in <u>formation</u>.

THERE ARE HOURS OF FUN TO BE HAD WITH YOUR FRIENDLY NEW PET!

GLOSSARY

ABSORB	to take in or soak up
AVIARY	structure designed for birds to live in
BONDING	forming a close relationship
ERA	a period of time in history
FORMATION	a particular arrangement of things or people
INLAND	part of a place that is away from the sea
NEST	any place used by an animal to lay eggs or rear young
PREDATORS	animals that hunt other animals for food

INDEX